A RAINBOW OF MY OWN

OF MY OWN

Don Freeman

Puffin Books

To
David

A share of the author's royalties from the sale of *A Rainbow of My Own*
goes to the *Don and Lydia Freeman Research Fund* to support psychological
research concerning children afflicted with cancer.

PUFFIN BOOKS
Published by the Penguin Group
Penguin Putnam Books for Young Readers, 345 Hudson Street, New York, New York 10014, U.S.A.
Penguin Books Ltd, 27 Wrights Lane, London W8 5TZ, England
Penguin Books Australia Ltd, Ringwood, Victoria, Australia
Penguin Books Canada Ltd, 10 Alcorn Avenue, Toronto, Ontario, Canada M4V 3B2
Penguin Books (N.Z.) Ltd, 182-190 Wairau Road, Auckland 10, New Zealand
Penguin Books Ltd, Registered Offices: Harmondsworth, Middlesex, England

First published by The Viking Press 1966
Viking Seafarer Edition published 1974
Published in Puffin Books 1978

45 46 47 48 49 50

Copyright © Don Freeman, 1966
All rights reserved

Library of Congress Cataloging in Publication Data
Freeman, Don   A rainbow of my own.
Summary: A small boy imagines what it would be
like to have his own rainbow to play with.
[1. Rainbow—Fiction.]   I. Title.
PZ7.8747Rai   1978   [E]   78-11136
ISBN 0 14 050.328 5

Manufactured in China

Today I saw a rainbow. It was so beautiful that I wanted to catch it for my very own.

I put on my raincoat and hat and ran outdoors.

Fast as the wind I ran.

But when I came to where the rainbow should have been,

it wasn't there.

I thought, Maybe some rainy day a rainbow will
come and stay a while. I'll be walking along slowly,

and suddenly I'll hear a soft whirring sound
like the wings of a bird. I'll look around and see

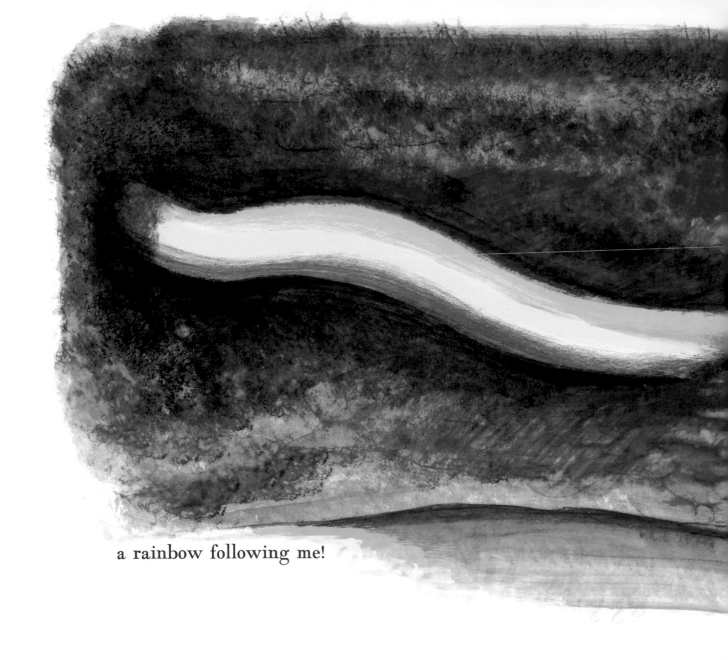

a rainbow following me!

I'll know by the way it circles and whirls

it wants to play.

So I'll hop over my rainbow,

and my rainbow will leap over me.

I'll climb up one side

and slide down the other.

My rainbow will make a peacock fan for me to walk in front of

and a hammock for me to swing in.

We'll play a game of hide-and-go-seek. I'll shut my eyes and count to twenty, and then look all around.

If I were a rainbow, where would I hide?

In a flower garden, of course!

Rows of flowers look like a rainbow.

Suddenly the sun came out again from behind the rain clouds,

and my pretend rainbow disappeared the way real rainbows do.

But when I came back home, I saw something glowing
inside the window of my room,

and when I ran indoors,

there was a rainbow dancing on the wall! The sun was shining through the water in my goldfish bowl, and it made a rainbow just for me—

a rainbow of my very own!